written by
KIRSTY APPLEBAUM

illustrated by
SAHAR HAGHGOO

PRINCESS MINNA

THE WICKED WOOD

D1477651

nosy crow

First published in the UK in 2023 by Nosy Crow Ltd
Wheat Wharf, 27a Shad Thames,
London, SE1 2XZ, UK

Nosy Crow Eireann Ltd
44 Orchard Grove, Kenmare,
Co Kerry, V93 FY22, Ireland

Nosy Crow and associated logos are trademarks and/or registered
trademarks of Nosy Crow Ltd.

Text copyright © Kirsty Applebaum, 2023
Cover and inside illustrations copyright © Sahar Haghgoo, 2023

The right of Kirsty Applebaum and Sahar Haghgoo to be identified
as the author and illustrator respectively of this work has been asserted
by them in accordance with the Copyright, Designs
and Patents Act 1988.

ISBN: 978 1 83994 942 5

A CIP catalogue record for this book will be available from the British Library.

Printed and bound in Poland.

Papers used by Nosy Crow are made from wood grown in sustainable forests.

1 3 5 7 9 10 8 6 4 2

www.nosycrow.com

Chapter
One

This is Minna. She is a **princess**. Princess Minna is very good at **lots** of things.

She is good at taming unicorns, kissing frogs and fighting dragons.

At weekends, Princess Minna loves to walk in The Enchanted Forest.

It's so beautiful!

Enchanted flowers **bloom** in the enchanted sunshine.

Enchanted butterflies **dance** in the enchanted air.

But Princess Minna is always careful not to wander too far. For beyond the Enchanted Forest lies the **Wicked Wood** ... and she doesn't like the sound of that,

not one little bit.

Princess Minna lives in Castle
Tall-Towers with the King, the
Queen and a wizard called
Raymond.

Lorenzo the dragon lives
in the castle garden.
He is Princess Minna's best
friend in the whole
world.

Castle Tall-Towers has some **very** tall towers. When all is well in the kingdom, lots of grey doves **sweep** and **swoop** around them making soft cooing noises. The doves make the whole castle smell like **tutti-frutti ice cream.**

When all is **not** well in the kingdom, big seagulls fly up from the coast and scare the doves away. Then they flip and flap around the towers, making **screechy, squawking** noises. They make the whole castle smell like **old seaweed.**

One morning, Princess Minna woke up to hear seagulls flipping and flapping outside her window.

Flip! Flap! Flap! Flip!

Oh dear, she thought. All is not
well in the kingdom. I'd better go
and find out what's wrong.

She ran **down**
and **down**
and **down**
and **down**
and **down**
and **down**

the stairs.

But when she got to the
bottom, the King and
Queen were **nowhere**
to be seen.

Princess Minna searched for the King and Queen **everywhere**. She searched in the royal kitchen, in the royal bathroom and in the royal bedroom.

13

She searched
behind all the royal
curtains,

underneath the royal sofa

and inside
the royal
laundry
basket.

The King and Queen were well
and truly

missing.

Not only that, but when Princess Minna went outside, she found that Lorenzo the dragon was missing too!

Raymond was **nowhere to be seen** either, but Princess Minna knew that was because he was on holiday.

Princess Minna ran all the way to the town.

"All is not well," she shouted. "The King, the Queen and Lorenzo are missing."

The townspeople clutched their hearts and frowned their frowns.

"Oh, what will we do?" they cried. "Oh, where can they be?"

Just then, some jolly woodcutters
passed by. They had been
doing some early-morning jolly
woodcutting.

"We saw them a few hours ago,"
they said. "They were flying over
the Enchanted Forest."

Princess Minna and the townspeople all breathed a **big** sigh of relief. The King, the Queen and Lorenzo were **safe**.

"They were heading for the Wicked Wood," added the jolly woodcutters.

The Wicked Wood?

The townspeople threw their hands to their faces. "Oh no!" they said. "The Wicked Wood is home to the **Wicked Witch** and the **wicked trees** and all kinds of **wicked creatures** who come out at night.

No one is safe
there at all."

21

Chapter Two

"Goodness," said Princess Minna.
"We must rescue the King, the
Queen and Lorenzo

straightaway."

But the Wicked Wood was
so creepy!

Princess Minna crossed her
fingers. She hoped that a brave
volunteer would step forward so
she wouldn't have to go herself.

"Fear not," said a small voice. It was Little Betty Button from Button's B shop. "I will rescue them in **no time at all**. Also, I will take a big bag of **brown breadcrumbs** from the B shop and leave a trail behind me as I go. That way we will easily be able to find our way home."

"Oh, thank you, Little Betty," cried Princess Minna.

So Little Betty ventured out of town, through the Enchanted Forest and towards the **Wicked Wood.** She left a trail of brown breadcrumbs behind her as she went.

"Fluttery birds!" called Little Betty. "Please don't peck at these breadcrumbs or my trail will be eaten away."

"We won't peck at your breadcrumbs," replied the fluttery birds.

Princess Minna and the townspeople waited ... and waited ... and waited.

Time ticked on, the day grew longer and the birds forgot their promise.

Little Betty's trail was **eaten completely away.**

"Oh dear," said Princess Minna.
"Now we must rescue the King, the
Queen, Lorenzo and Little Betty."

But the Wicked Wood was
so eerie! Princess Minna crossed
her fingers **and her arms.**
She hoped that another brave
volunteer would step forward so
she wouldn't have to go herself.

"Fear not," said a small voice. It was Little Tommy Turret from Turret's T shop. "I will rescue them in **no time at all**. Also, I will take a titanic tub of **tiny tomatoes** from the T shop and leave a trail behind me as I go. It's sure to last **much** longer than breadcrumbs."

"Oh, thank you, Little Tommy," cried Princess Minna.

So Little Tommy ventured out of town, through the Enchanted Forest and towards the Wicked Wood. He left a trail of tiny tomatoes behind him as he went.

"Hoppity hares!" called Little Tommy. "Please don't nibble these tomatoes or my trail will be munched away."

"We won't nibble your tomatoes," replied the hoppity hares.

Princess Minna and the townspeople waited ... and waited ... and waited.

Time ticked on, the day grew
longer and the hares forgot
their promise.

Little Tommy's trail
was **munched
completely away.**

"Oh dear," said Princess Minna.
"Now we must rescue the King,
the Queen, Lorenzo, Little Betty
and Little Tommy."

But the Wicked Wood was
so spooky!

Princess Minna crossed her
fingers and her arms and her
legs. She hoped that yet another
brave volunteer would step
forward so she wouldn't have to
go herself.

"Fear not," said a small voice. It was Little Pippi Piper from Piper's P shop. "I will rescue them in **no time at all**. Also, I will take a plentiful packet of **pink popcorn** from the P shop and leave a trail behind me as I go. It's sure to last much longer than breadcrumbs **or** tomatoes."

"Oh, thank you, Little Pippi," cried Princess Minna.

So Little Pippi ventured out of town, through the Enchanted Forest and towards the **Wicked Wood**. She left a trail of pink popcorn behind her as she went.

"Gusty wind!" called Little Pippi.
"Please don't blow on this popcorn
or my trail will be whisked away."
"I won't blow on your popcorn,"
replied the gusty wind.

Princess Minna and the
townspeople waited ...
and waited ...
and waited.

Time ticked on, the day grew longer and the wind forgot its promise.

Little Pippi's trail was **whisked completely away**.

Chapter Three

"**Oh no!**" cried the townspeople.

"The day has grown

very long indeed."

"What will happen to the King and Queen?"

"What will happen to Little Betty, Little Tommy and Little Pippi?"

"What will happen to Lorenzo?"

"If they're not rescued by
sundown, they'll have to **sleep**
in the Wicked Wood ... with the
Wicked Witch ... and the
wicked trees ... and the
wicked creatures who come
out at night!"

42

43

Princess Minna took a big, deep, **brave** breath. "There's only one thing for it," she said. "I must **conquer my fear** and venture into the Wicked Wood myself — and I must do it quickly."

"Hurrah!"

cried the townspeople.

Princess Minna hurried out of the town towards the Enchanted Forest, but in her rush she completely forgot to leave a trail of anything at all.

Princess Minna didn't mind walking through the Enchanted Forest. The enchanted trees smiled kindly at her and waved their **enchanted branches.**

But as she walked
further, the trees became

gloomy

and

scary.

I must be in the
Wicked Wood now,
thought Princess Minna.
And these must be the
wicked trees.

51

She tried not to look at their **creepy** tangled branches.
She tried not to touch their **eerie** twisted trunks.
She tried not to listen to their **spooky** rustling leaves.

52

"Be brave, Princess Minna,"
she told herself. "Keep going."
She had to find everyone
before it was **too late**.

Chapter
Four

Although the wicked trees loomed
and groaned and scowled, they
allowed Princess Minna safe
passage through the wood.
Presently, she came to a clearing.

"Gosh," she said in surprise.

In the middle of the clearing was a house. But this house wasn't made of bricks or wood or stone. It was made **entirely of lemony gingerbread.**

Even the **wheelie bin** was made of lemony gingerbread. It smelled delicious.

And look! The King,
Lorenzo, Little Betty, Little
Tommy and Little Pippi were all
chomping away at different bits
of the house.

The Queen was sitting on the grass, looking a bit fed up. "Oh!" she said. "Thank goodness you're here, Minna."

"I'm so glad I was brave enough to come and find you," said Princess Minna. "Now everything will be all right."

But then...

57

Creeeeeeeeak!

The front door of the lemony gingerbread house swung open. There stood a little old lady who looked as gloomy and scary as the wicked trees themselves.

It was the Wicked Witch!

"**Wicked Witch**," cried Princess Minna. "Please release the King, the Queen, Lorenzo, Little Betty, Little Tommy and Little Pippi **this minute!**"

The Wicked Witch
seemed confused.
"Do you mean me?"
she said.
"Yes!" said
Princess Minna.
"You captured all these
prisoners. You're the
Wicked Witch!"
"I didn't capture
anyone," said the
Wicked Witch, "and
although I am a **witch**,
I'm not **wicked**."

"Then why do you look as gloomy and scary as the wicked trees themselves?" said Princess Minna.

"**You'd** look gloomy and scary if people kept eating **your** house," said the witch.

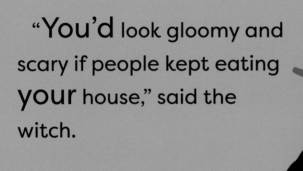

"It's true," said the Queen.
"This lady has done nothing wrong.

The King woke me up this morning saying he could smell the most wonderful lemony gingerbread

in the world.

We asked Lorenzo to help us track it down. Since then, they have both been **eating** and **eating** and I can't get them to leave. Then Little Betty, Little Tommy and Little Pippi turned up and they won't stop **eating** either. There was a double garage next to the house this morning. They've gobbled it all up."

"Mmmm," said Princess Minna. "The gingerbread does smell **very** nice.

But we have to go. It's not safe here. Look at all the wicked trees."

"Actually," said the Queen, "the trees are quite friendly. I've been chatting to them for most of the day."

67

"The **trees** aren't wicked," said the witch, "and neither am I. But the wicked creatures are **definitely wicked.** So, if you'll excuse me, I'm going inside. It's almost **night-time.**"

With that, she stepped back into her house and pulled the front door tightly shut.

68

Princess Minna looked up.
The witch was right. Day was
at its end and the wicked
creatures would very soon be

out.

Chapter Five

"We need to leave

right now!"

said Princess Minna. "Which way is home?"

"This way," said the Queen.

"No, it's this way," said the King.

"Maybe it's that way," said Little
Betty.

"Or that way," said Little Tommy.

"Or that way," said Little Pippi.

Everyone was pointing in different directions, but which was the right one?

They were completely **lost**.

"How will we **ever** find our way back?" cried Little Betty, Little Tommy and Little Pippi.

"I know!" said Princess Minna. "Lorenzo can carry us all home. We'll be able to see our way as soon as we're up in the air."

So, as darkness closed in, everyone climbed on to the dragon's back.

Lorenzo spread his wings, took a breath and ...

nothing happened.

74

He had eaten **so much lemony gingerbread** that he couldn't get off the ground.

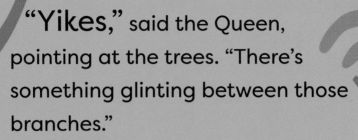

"Yikes," said the Queen, pointing at the trees. "There's something glinting between those branches."

"It looks like wicked eyes!" said Little Betty.

"And wicked teeth!" said Little Tommy.

"And wicked claws!" said Little Pippi.

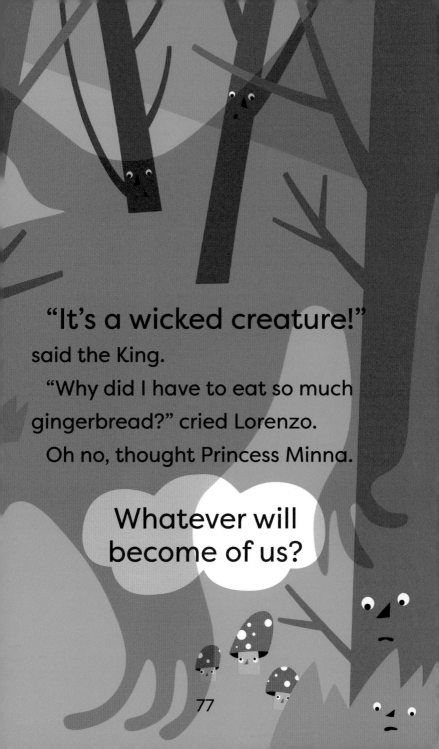

"It's a wicked creature!" said the King.

"Why did I have to eat so much gingerbread?" cried Lorenzo.

Oh no, thought Princess Minna.

Whatever will become of us?

77

But then she had a
marvellous idea.

"Don't worry, everyone,"
said Princess Minna. "I've thought
up a plan."

"Fluttery birds!" she called out.
"Hoppity hares! Gusty wind! Will
you help us?"

The fluttery birds **fluttered** down from the branches.

The **hoppity hares hopped** out from the bushes.

The gusty wind **gusted** in from the sky.

79

"Of course we'll help!"
they all said.

"Oh, thank you," said Princess
Minna. "We're having trouble
taking off."

So the fluttery birds took hold
of Lorenzo in their beaks ...

... and the hoppity hares pushed
Lorenzo with their paws ...

... and the gusty wind gathered
itself under Lorenzo's wings.

Then all at once the birds
fluttered and the hares
hopped and the wind
gusted and ...

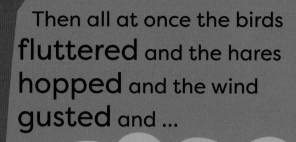

wallooop!

They were off!

Up, up, up they flew ...
away from the wicked **eyes**
and the wicked **teeth**
and the wicked **claws** ...

and soon they were

safely home.

Back at Castle Tall-Towers the doves were cooing softly. Everywhere smelled like tutti-frutti ice cream. There wasn't a seagull in sight.

The King, the Queen and Princess Minna sat down on the **royal sofa**. They heard a key in the **royal front door**.

And all was well in the kingdom once more.

It was Raymond, home from his holiday.

"I had a brilliant time," he said. "Look, I've brought you all a present." He pulled something out of his bag.

It was a **huge tin** of lemony gingerbread.

"Oh, no!" said Princess Minna, laughing.